Sometimes teasing can be fun and playful. But if someone's teasing makes you feel upset, that's emotional bullying. Emotional bullying can also include taunting, humiliation, spreading rumours and ganging up on others.

5

"Go on! Take it!" Sam slides the dirty comb into my pocket.

I don't know what to do. Everyone is watching.

"You could say thank you," Sam says.

"Poor people have bad manners," says Jesse. "They're ugly too."

I feel like an insect. A tiny, awful insect.

The bus arrives, and I step closer to the kerb.
The door opens. Sam and Jesse push ahead of me.

"Beauty before ugly," Jesse says loudly.

I climb on behind them. They go to the back seat. The only spare seats are near them. I take a deep breath and sit next to Erin. Erin slides away from me, closer to the window.

It's like I have a disease no one wants to catch.

Things are quiet for a while. My shoulders drop a little. Maybe it will be OK now.

Then Sam yells, **"Who's the ugliest kid at school?"**

About 46 per cent of children experience bullying before the age of 18.

Jesse chants, **"Ug-ly Nat!"**

A few other kids join in. **"Ug-ly Nat!"**

My face burns. I want to disappear.

The bus finally arrives at school. I climb off as fast as I can.

Someone is walking next to me. Oh no.
Now what?

"Nat?"

I look over. It's Alex. Alex is in my class.

"Hi," Alex says. "I just want to say it's not right the way those kids treat you. It's mean. And you're not ugly. I hope you don't believe them."

I didn't know anyone cared. I hold back tears. **"Thanks."**

"Have you told anyone?" Alex asks. "Like your parents or Mr West?"

Mr West is our teacher. I shake my head no. Sam and Jesse are really popular. I'm too ashamed to tell anyone what they say about me.

"Well," Alex says, "it's just an idea. But I'm sure an adult can help if you say something." Alex smiles.

A simple way to help someone who's being bullied is to make him or her feel included. Say hello in the playground or sit with him or her at lunchtime.

Alex seems to understand what I'm going through.
All day I think about what Alex said. Sam and Jesse
are mean. I'm *not* ugly. It's *not* right.

After break time, I see the headteacher, Ms Mills, in the corridor. I like Ms Mills. She's friendly to everyone.

"Hello, Nat," she says. **"How are you?"**

I stop in front of her.

"Nat?" she asks. **"Is something wrong?"**

I nod. **"Can I talk to you?"**

Ms Mills takes me to her office. **"Tell me what's upsetting you."**

I tell her that kids are mean to me, especially on the bus.

"In what way are they mean?" she asks.

It's hard to tell her, but I do. I hope she believes me.

"I'm sorry this is happening to you, Nat," she says. **"And I'm glad you told me. You're being bullied. We don't allow children from our school to be bullies, not even on the bus."** Ms Mills says she'll talk to Sam and Jesse and the bus driver.

That scares me. "They'll think I told on them," I say. "It will make things worse."

"You leave that to me," Ms Mills says with a reassuring smile. "In the meantime, do you have a friend on the bus you can sit with?"

"No," I answer. Then I think about Alex. "Well, maybe."

After school I see Alex heading for our bus. I run and catch up.

"I talked to Ms Mills," I say.

"Great!" Alex says. **"I bet you feel better."**

I think about it. I *do* feel better. It's like my shoulders aren't so heavy.

Children who have at least one friend are less likely to be bullied than children without any friends.

19

We get on the bus. I hear Sam and Jesse laughing from the back seat.

"Alex?" I ask. "Is it OK if I sit with you?"

"As long as you don't mind sitting at the front," Alex says. "I used to get teased a lot. Staying near the bus driver helps."

Alex and I talk on the way home. I tell Alex about my hamster, Gus. Alex walks dogs at an animal shelter. It sounds like fun. **"You can come with me one day,"** Alex says. **"They always need volunteers."**

Taking part in a fun activity outside of school, such as a sport, club or volunteering, is a great way to make friends and feel better about yourself.

The bus arrives at my stop. I get an idea.

"Alex?" I ask. "Do you want to sit together on the bus in the morning?"

"Absolutely!" Alex says with a wave. "See you tomorrow."

"Great! See you tomorrow." I wave back.

If Sam and Jesse have been talking about me, I can't hear them. And I don't care. I've made a new friend today.